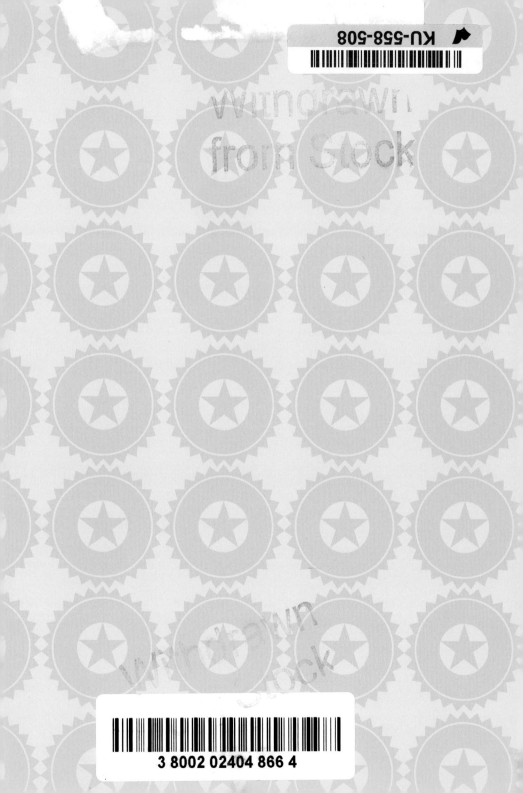

The Pied
Piper Returns

by Jenny Jinks and Hannah George

FRANKLIN WATTS
LONDON•SYDNEY

Chapter 1

"Get down!" shouted Ash's mum.

"It's far too dangerous!"

Ash ignored her and hurried up the last few steps

to the top of the slide.

As he slid to the bottom of the slide,

Mum grabbed his arm. "Right, that's it," she said.

"We're going home. Don't you realise what could

have happened? You could have fallen. You could

have hurt yourself!"

For lunch, Ash's mum gave him a super healthy salad. Chopped into bite-sized pieces, of course, so Ash wouldn't choke. It was fat-free, danger-free, and ... taste-free.

Ash wasn't allowed to do anything fun any more. Not since the mysterious Pied Piper had visited Hamelin. When the town had been overrun with rats, the Piper had played his pipe and led all the rats away. But when the mayor refused to pay him, the Piper had led all the children away, too.

The townspeople raised the money to pay the Piper, and the children came back with no memory of their time away. But the townspeople had never forgotten. They were determined not to let anything happen to their children again. In fact, they had gone safety-mad.

5

Chapter 2

"We have to do something!" complained Mala.

"I haven't been allowed out all day!"

"I've completely forgotten what cake, ice cream
and biscuits taste like," moaned Freddie, holding
his stomach.

The friends were holding a secret meeting in
Ash's treehouse. They were not allowed there
during the day. It was "much too dangerous"
his mum had said.

Freddie pulled out the box stuffed full of sweets that they had hidden in the treehouse. Every night, they shared out their rations and discussed what to do about their parents.

"I wish we didn't have to listen to their ridiculous rules," grumbled Ash.

"I wish we didn't have to listen to them at all!" said Mala.

Just then they heard some strange music coming from outside. A man in a colourful cloak was sitting on a branch, playing a pipe. His eyes twinkled as brightly as the stars above.

Ash recognised the man straight away.

"I remember you," he said in surprise.

"You're the Pied Piper," gasped Freddie.

"I seem to have caused you some trouble,"

the Piper said. "I'm here to solve your problem."

Chapter 3

"Can you solve our parent problem?"

asked Ash.

The Piper nodded. "All I ask is a little something

in return," he said.

"But we don't have any money," Mala said.

The Piper thought for a moment.

His eyes flicked to the box of delicious treats

clutched tightly in Freddie's hands.

"You could give me your sweets," the Piper said.

"Our sweets?" said Freddie "No way.

They are the only good things we have left!"

"Do you want my help or not?" the Piper asked.

"If I take your parents away, then you can eat all

the sweets you want."

The three friends huddled together.

"Can we trust him?" whispered Mala.

"Think of the sweets!" said Freddie, longingly.

"I don't know ..." said Ash.

But when they looked up, the Piper had gone.

Chapter 4

If the three friends thought things
couldn't get any worse,
they were wrong.
Ash's mum got rid of the
TV. "It's bad for
your eyes!" she told him.

And now Freddie had to sleep on the floor.

"Can't have you falling out of bed!" his dad said.

"I haven't had a wink of sleep," Freddie yawned, at their next meeting. "I'm so tired."

"It's getting ridiculous," said Mala, as she passed the sweets round.

"These won't last us much longer," Ash said, looking in the nearly empty box.

"I think we need the Piper's help," said Freddie.

Then they heard the Piper's music outside.

"Please, we want you to sort out our parents,"

the friends said. "We'll give you anything."

The Piper's eyes twinkled. Without a word, he left,

playing his pipe as he went.

One by one, front doors opened. The parents came out listening to the Piper's music and followed the Piper down the road. He led them right out of town, up into the hills.

The friends couldn't believe their eyes.

The Piper had done it – their parents were gone!

Chapter 5

The next morning, Ash woke up late. Why hadn't his mum woken him? Then he remembered. No parents! Ash and his friends had the best day. They ate nothing but sweets and chocolate.

When they ran out, they went to the shop.

"But we don't have any money," said Mala.

"There are no adults," said Freddie.

"We can take what

we want!"

They ate sweets and played in the park until

the sun set. Then they watched TV until their eyes

were sore.

Then they heard the familiar music outside.

"I did what you wanted. Now where's my payment?" the Piper asked.

"We don't have any sweets," said Mala, quickly.

"We've eaten them all," said Freddie, hiding some behind his back.

"You'll be sorry that you didn't pay

when you had the chance," said the Piper,

his eyes twinkling even brighter.

And then he was gone.

"Why would we be sorry?" said Ash.

"Life is great!"

But life wasn't great for long. The friends didn't know how to cook or clean. Ash's house was a mess in no time. There was no food in the cupboards. Everything began to smell. Soon the friends had all had enough.

"I'm hungry," said Ash.

"We could get some more sweets?" suggested Mala.

"I never want another sweet ever again," Freddie groaned, holding his tummy. "Have we got any carrots left?"

"These won't last us much longer," said Ash, looking in the box that they now used to hold fruit and vegetables. "I think it's time to get our parents back."

Ash, Mala and Freddie collected all the sweets
they could find and walked up into the hills.
It was the last place they had seen their parents.
"Pied Piper, we're sorry," shouted Ash. There was
no response.

"We didn't mean what we said," said Mala.

"Please can we have our parents back?"

"We have your sweets," said Freddie, hopefully.

But the Piper and the parents still didn't appear.

How were they going to survive without them?

The next morning Ash woke to the smell of hot porridge. He ran downstairs. "Mum!" he cried.

"Morning Ash," his mum said. Everything was normal, like she had never left. She put a steaming bowl of plain porridge in front of him.

"Here you go," she said. "It's hot. Be careful you don't burn your mouth."

Everything was normal. But Ash was so happy
to have his mum back he didn't complain.
"Fancy going to the park later?" she said.
Ash blinked in disbelief. Maybe things were better
after all.

Ash and his friends held another meeting that night in the treehouse.

"Dad cooked eleven types of vegetable for tea," said Freddie, grinning.

"Mum folded the corners on my book so I wouldn't get a paper cut," Mala said, happily.

Outside the Piper smiled, his eyes twinkling like the stars above. He played softly on his pipe. And then he was gone.

Things to think about

1. Why are the adults so protective of their children?
2. How do Ash, Mala and Freddie feel when the adults have vanished? Does life seem better?
3. Why do the friends change their mind about the adults?
4. Why don't the children keep their end of the bargain?
5. What similarities and differences are there with the original fairy tale about the Pied Piper? What are the main themes of this version?

Write it yourself

One of the themes in this story is being careful what you wish for. Now try to write your own story with a similar theme.

Plan your story before you begin to write it.

Start off with a story map:

• a beginning to introduce the characters and where and when your story is set (the setting);

• a problem which the main characters will need to fix in the story;

• an ending where the problems are resolved.

Get writing! Try to have dramatic or unexpected twists to your plot to keep the reader guessing what will happen. Use energetic language with exclamations!

Notes for parents and carers

Independent reading
The aim of independent reading is to read this book with ease. This series is designed to provide an opportunity for your child to read for pleasure and enjoyment. These notes are written for you to help your child make the most of this book.

About the book
The town of Hamelin has changed a lot since the Pied Piper last visited. The parents have gone safety-mad and the children are not allowed to do anything —including eat sweets! Ash and his friends have had enough. So when the Pied Piper pops back, they know just what to wish for ... a world without adults!

Before reading
Ask your child why they have selected this book. Look at the title and blurb together. What do they think it will be about? Do they think they will like it?

During reading
Encourage your child to read independently. If they get stuck on a longer word, remind them that they can find syllable chunks that can be sounded out from left to right. They can also read on in the sentence and think about what would make sense.

After reading
Support comprehension by talking about the story. What happened?
Then help your child think about the messages in the book that go beyond the story, using the questions on the page opposite. Give your child a chance to respond to the story, asking:
Did you enjoy the story and why? Who was your favourite character?
What was your favourite part? What did you expect to happen at the end?

Franklin Watts
First published in Great Britain in 2018
by The Watts Publishing Group

Series Editors: Jackie Hamley and Melanie Palmer
Series Advisors: Dr Sue Bodman and Glen Franklin
Series Designer: Peter Scoulding

A CIP catalogue record for this book is
available from the British Library.

ISBN 978 1 4451 6335 2 (hbk)
ISBN 978 1 4451 6337 6 (pbk)
ISBN 978 1 4451 6336 9 (library ebook)

Printed in China

Franklin Watts
An imprint of
Hachette Children's Group
Part of The Watts Publishing Group
Carmelite House
50 Victoria Embankment
London EC4Y 0DZ

An Hachette UK Company
www.hachette.co.uk

www.franklinwatts.co.uk